D1172233

Arabella
and the
Magic Pencil

STEPHANIE WARD & SHANEY HYDE

First published 2019

EK Books
an imprint of Exisle Publishing Pty Ltd
PO Box 864, Chatswood, NSW 2057, Australia
226 High Street, Dunedin, 9016, New Zealand
www.ekbooks.org

Copyright © 2019 in text: Stephanie Ward
Copyright © 2019 in illustrations: Shaney Hyde

Stephanie Ward & Shaney Hyde assert the moral right to be identified as the creators of this work.

All rights reserved. Except for short extracts for the purpose of review, no part of this book may be reproduced, stored in a retrieval system or transmitted in any form or by any means, whether electronic, mechanical, photocopying, recording or otherwise, without prior written permission from the publisher.

A CiP record for this book is available from the National Library of Australia.

ISBN 978-1-925820-01-0

Designed by Big Cat Design
Typeset in Minya Nouvelle 17/24pt
Printed in China

This book uses paper sourced under ISO 14001 guidelines from well-managed forests and other controlled sources.

10 9 8 7 6 5 4 3 2 1

To every child who became a big brother or big sister.

— S.W.

For my beautiful mum.

— S.H.

Arabella
and the
Magic Pencil

There once
was a girl named
Arabella.

She was the only child of a
duke and duchess who doted
on their delightful daughter.

By royal decree, Arabella was granted one wish each year.

She wished for splendid things ...

A pink puppy.

An amusement park.

A real-life faery.

She did not wish for a brother.

But Arabella did get a brother.
Master Archibald Vermillion Remington XV,
or Avery for short.

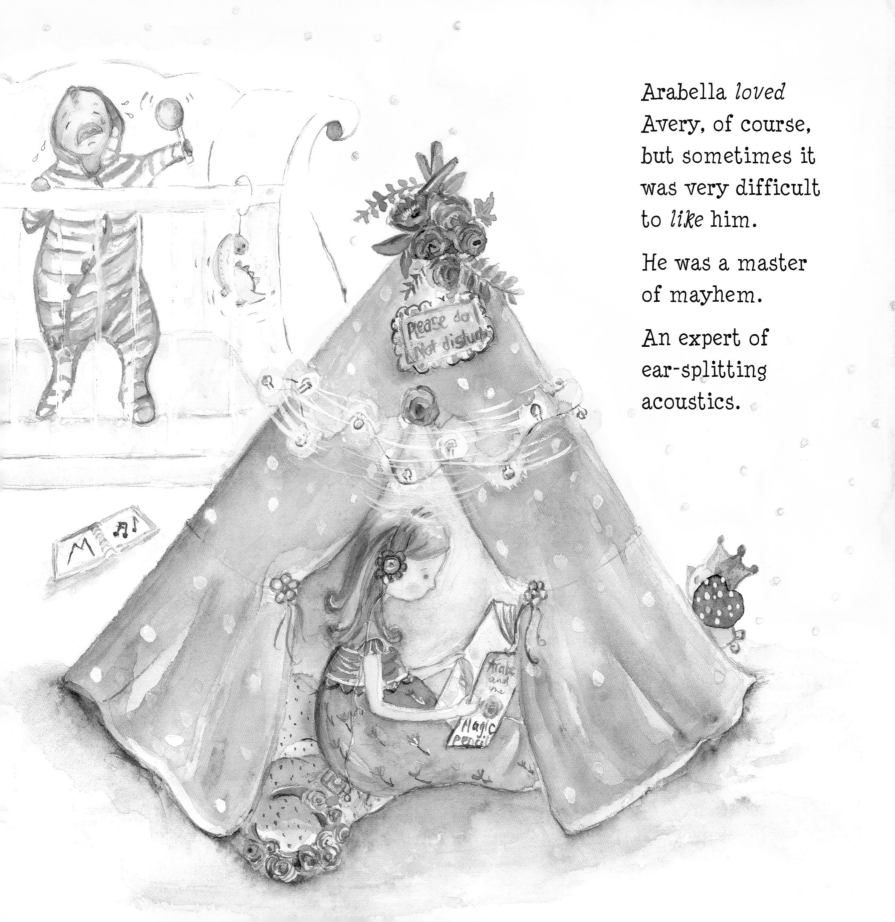

Arabella *loved* Avery, of course, but sometimes it was very difficult to *like* him.

He was a master of mayhem.

An expert of ear-splitting acoustics.

An ace at
annoying
Arabella.

When the time came for her next wish,
Arabella asked for a magic pencil — one that
could make anything she drew become real.

She coloured flowers that could sing.

She sketched
a flying bicycle.

And the fuzzy,
rainbow-striped hippo
she drew for a pet
was undoubtedly
one of a kind.

One particularly imaginative day, Arabella created a magnificent garden tea party.

Dainty dolls dined.

Pretty princesses paraded.

Flashy flamingos flamencoed.

And this jolly jamboree took place next to
a spectacular ice-cream sundae mountain.

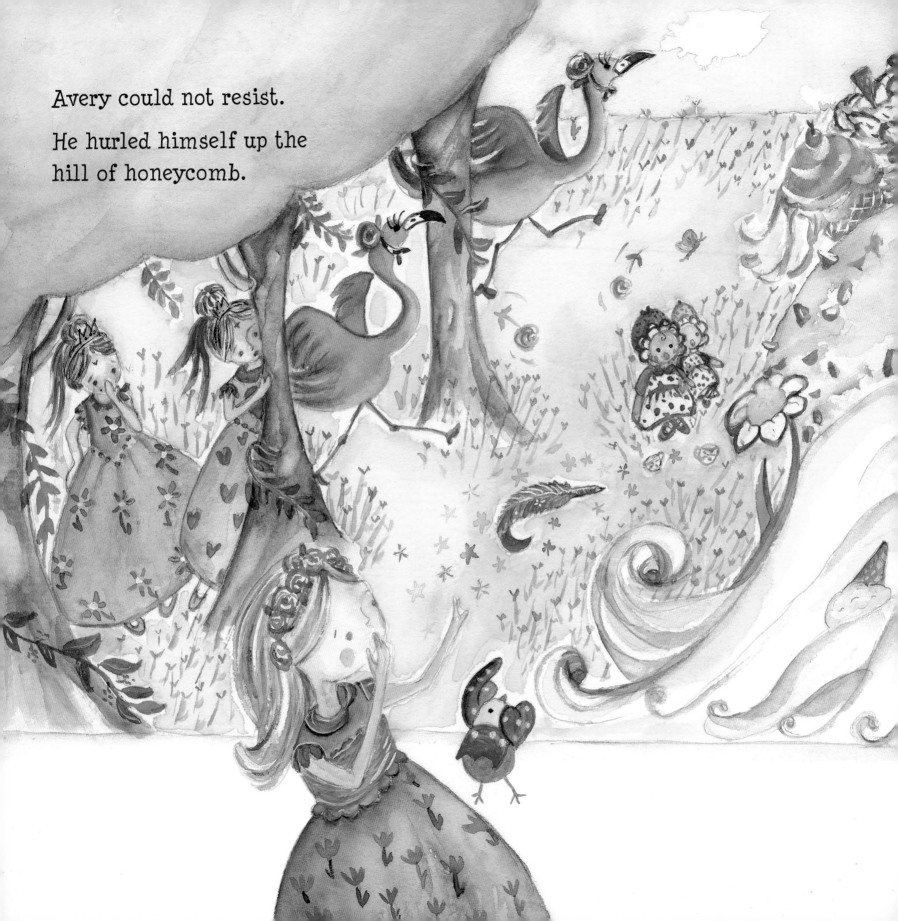

Avery could not resist.

He hurled himself up the
hill of honeycomb.

Skipped across the sparkly sprinkles.

Wallowed in the whipped-cream waterfall.

'Stop this minute!' cried Arabella. But Avery was busy bouncing on bubble gum boulders.

'Avery, you've ruined everything!' she screamed.

Arabella flew up the mountain, pulled
Avery out of the faery floss forest, took
out her magic pencil and ...

... erased him — from the tip of his nose to the end of his toes.

Avery was gone.

It was quiet.

It was calm.

It was just as a
tea party should be.

But Arabella did not feel
any better.

It was *too* quiet.

Too calm.

Too un-Avery like!

'What have I done?' sobbed
Arabella, sinking with sadness.
'How can I get my brother back?'

Then she pictured Avery
in her mind and she
knew just what to do.

For hours, Arabella worked on her finest drawing.

She carefully sketched Avery's sparkling eyes. His sweet nose. His bright smile. She brushed his golden hair with the tip of her pencil and lightly feathered his long eyelashes.

When she had finished,
Arabella put down the magic
pencil and closed her eyes.

When she opened them ...

... Avery was there.

Just like he had been.

Just like he was supposed to be.

Arabella was so
happy to have Avery
back that she drew
a very special gift
for him.

And she promised never to erase him again.

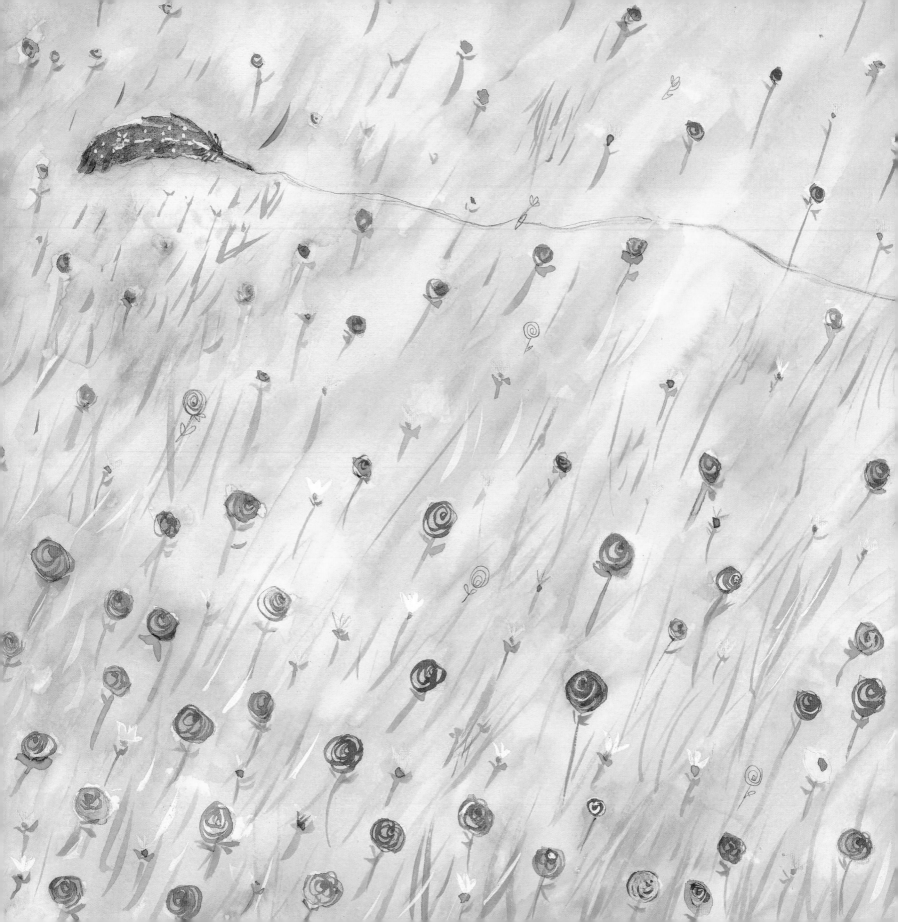